The Paradise Garden

Colin Thompson

RED FOX

All day and all night and all around it roared.

Only in one place was there any peace. In the west of the city was a fabulous garden. There, behind its tall walls and thick trees it was possible to escape the noise. For Peter, who had lived all his life in narrow streets, it was the closest place to paradise he had ever seen.

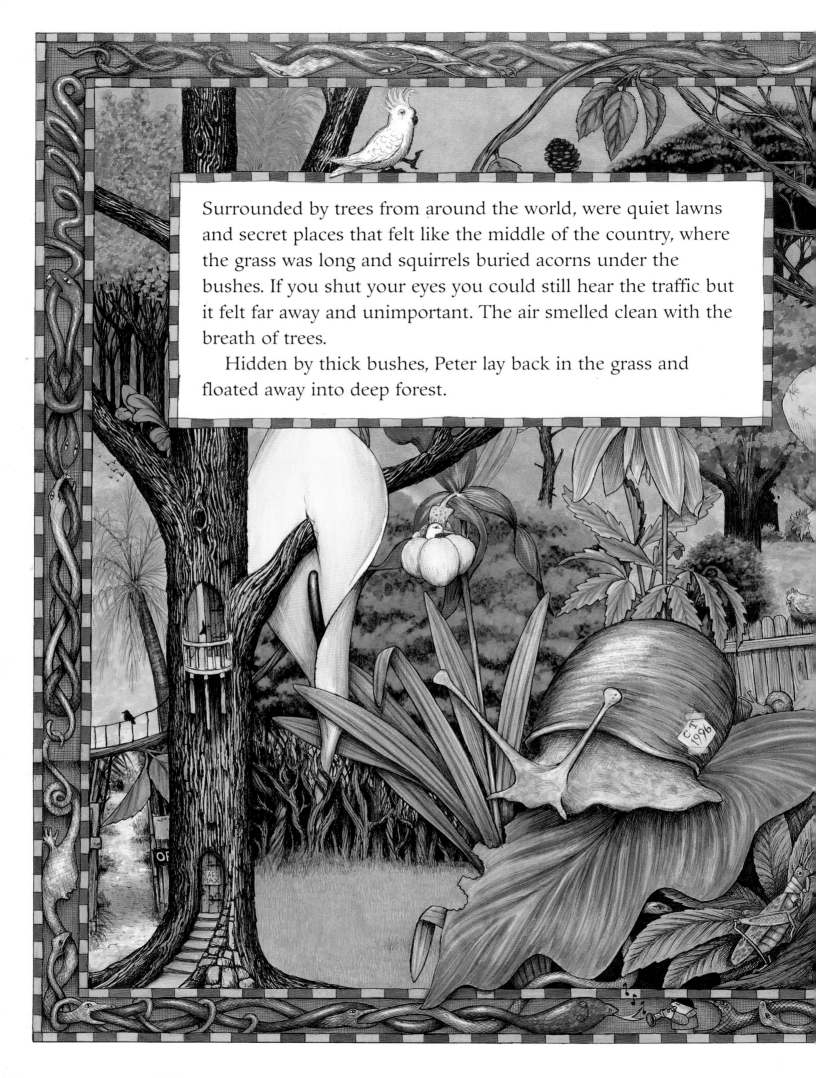

Surrounded by trees from around the world, were quiet lawns and secret places that felt like the middle of the country, where the grass was long and squirrels buried acorns under the bushes. If you shut your eyes you could still hear the traffic but it felt far away and unimportant. The air smelled clean with the breath of trees.

Hidden by thick bushes, Peter lay back in the grass and floated away into deep forest.

He'd planned his escape so no one would miss him. It was simple. He told his mother he was going on holiday with his father. She was annoyed, but not enough to stop him, not enough to phone his father.

That night Peter slept beneath the stars. The city had dropped to a faint murmur. Foxes hunted through the garden and owls called out in the dark. No monsters visited Peter's dreams that night. There were no nightmares of running through slowed-down time, just peaceful empty sleep.

The first weeks were wonderful. He thought he might get fed up with the garden, that maybe its magic would wear off, but it didn't. He thought about his sister and his friends. He thought about his parents fighting and his father walking out. It all seemed so far away. It was as if the garden wall were a boundary to another world.

He bought food in the cafés and washed his clothes in a lotus pond among tall bamboos. And as he went through the garden he collected things: a gold ring, a red balloon and pocketfuls of seeds.

And when it rained, there were the great glass houses. Beneath their crystal skies it was forever summer. At night Peter crept into the Palm House to pick bananas and exotic fruits from around the world.

He grew to know every part of the garden, from quiet forgotten pathways where lovers walked to wide paths of bright flowers where old ladies sat and painted.

He grew to know the animals too. At home he had never been allowed a cat or a dog or even a fish, but here he had dozens of friends.

Eventually his money and the bananas ran out and he had to live on other people's leftovers. But even then he was happy. No one shouted at him. No one told him he was stupid. No one tried to make him do things he couldn't. And no one made him face up to the fact that he would have to go home one day.

Life was so peaceful.

At night he climbed the tallest tree and looked out at the distant city sparkling like fallen stars.

He walked between tropical palms and swam with brilliant goldfish in a pool of giant waterlilies.

In a corner of the garden, behind tall brick walls, was the only house where people lived.

Peter stood in the shadows by the window and watched the family inside. A fire burned in the grate, turning the room into gold.

Two children played cards on the floor while their parents watched television and on the carpet an old dog dreamed of its youth. Peter felt a terrible sadness in his heart, a deep loneliness that he realised had been there all his short life.

Summer grew weary. Everything slowed down and stopped growing. A fine dust covered the leaves.

The flowers turned their heads to the ground and Peter felt lonely. The leaves turned gold and began to fall and Peter knew it was time to go home.

In the yard behind his house Peter planted all the seeds he had collected. Nothing at home had changed. The noise still went on day and night. His mother shouted, the neighbours shouted and the city roared. But now he had his own paradise garden, and knew that he would always have one wherever he went.

For Anne
who brought me peace

With special thanks to Chris
and everyone at The Royal Botanic Gardens, Kew

A Red Fox Book

Published by Random House Children's Books
20 Vauxhall Bridge Road, London SW1V 2SA

A division of The Random House Group Ltd
London Melbourne Sydney Auckland
Johannesburg and agencies throughout the world

Copyright © Colin Thompson 1998

1 3 5 7 9 10 8 6 4 2

First published in Great Britain by Jonathan Cape Ltd 1998

Red Fox edition 2001

Printed and bound in Singapore by Tien Wah Press (PTE) Ltd.

THE RANDOM HOUSE GROUP Limited Reg. No. 954009

www.randomhouse.co.uk

ISBN 0 09 960921 5

Visit Colin Thompson's home page at
http://www.colinthompson.com